DATE DUE

P9-DUT-916

Pumas
Lone Hunters

Amelie von Zumbusch

PowerKiDS
press
New York

Published in 2007 by The Rosen Publishing Group, Inc.
29 East 21st Street, New York, NY 10010

First Edition

Book Design: Erica Clendening
Layout Design: Julio Gil
Photo Researcher: Sam Cha

Photo Credits: Cover, p. 1 © www.istockphoto.com/Vlado Marinkovic; p. 4 © www.istockphoto.com/moodville; pp. 6, 14, 16 © www.shutterstock.com; p. 8 U.S. Fish and Wildlife Service. Photo by George Gentry; pp. 10, 20 © Digital Vision; p. 12 © www.istockphoto.com/Jurie Maree; p. 18 U.S. Fish and Wildlife Service. Photo by USFWS.

Library of Congress Cataloging-in-Publication Data

Zumbusch, Amelie von.
  Pumas : lone hunters / Amelie von Zumbusch. — 1st ed.
      p. cm. — (Dangerous cats)
  Includes index.
  ISBN-13: 978-1-4042-3629-5 (library binding)
  ISBN-10: 1-4042-3629-5 (library binding)
  1. Puma—Juvenile literature. I. Title.
  QL737.C23Z798 2007
  599.75'24—dc22
                                        2006019528

Manufactured in the United States of America

Contents

The Puma

The puma is a member of the cat family. Pumas are large, strong animals. Pumas weigh between 80 and 225 pounds (36–102 kg). They are between 3 and 6 feet (1–2 m) long. However, pumas cannot roar, as great cats, such as lions and tigers, do. Instead pumas **yowl**, purr, or **hiss**.

Pumas are known by several different names. Many people call pumas mountain lions or cougars. Other people call them catamounts or panthers.

The word "puma" comes from the Quechua language. Quechua is a Native American language from South America.

An American Cat

Pumas live in North America, Central America, and South America. Pumas used to live throughout North America. However, most of the pumas in the eastern parts of Canada and the United States have died out. A few pumas remain in Florida, but most pumas in the United States and Canada live in the West.

Pumas can live in many different **habitats**. Some pumas live in thick forests. Other pumas live on dry, rocky mountains.

This puma lives on a grassland. Pumas can also live in other habitats, such as forests or deserts.

Different Kinds of Pumas

There are more than 20 **subspecies** of pumas. Different subspecies of pumas often live in different places. For example, the Texas cougar lives in the southern United States. The Patagonian puma lives in southern South America. It is one of the largest kinds of puma.

The Florida panther is another subspecies of puma. It lives in the southeastern United States. **Scientists** believe that there are fewer than 100 Florida panthers alive today.

This Florida panther lives in the wetlands of Florida.

What Pumas Look Like

Pumas have plain brown or gray coats. All pumas have lighter fur on their stomach. They have darker fur around their nose and at the end of their tail. Pumas have long, strong tails. A puma's tail is 2 to 3 feet (.6–1 m) long.

As all cats do, pumas have **whiskers** below their nose. Pumas can feel small movements in the air around them with their whiskers. Pumas also see and hear well.

Many pumas have white fur around their mouth.

11

Jumping Pumas

Pumas have powerful bodies. They have very strong back legs. A puma's back legs are longer than its front legs. These back legs make pumas excellent jumpers.

Pumas are some of the best jumpers in the cat family. A puma can go 40 feet (12 m) in just one **leap**! Pumas also jump up into trees. A puma can leap up onto a tree branch 18 feet (5 m) above the ground.

Pumas are also good at climbing trees.

A Powerful Hunter

As all wild cats are, pumas are **predators**. Pumas in different places hunt different animals for food. Pumas in the United States eat mostly deer. They also catch smaller animals, such as rabbits and raccoons.

Pumas hide behind rocks or bushes and creep up on their **prey**. Once a puma is close enough, it leaps on the animal it is hunting. The puma kills its prey by biting it with its sharp teeth.

Pumas creep up on their prey quietly and carefully.

Puma Kittens

Just as baby house cats are, baby pumas are called kittens. Puma kittens are born with spotted fur. They lose their spots when they are about six months old.

Puma kittens are born with their eyes closed. The kittens do not open their eyes until they are about 10 days old. Young pumas have bluish eyes. A puma's eyes will turn brown or gold when it is fully grown.

Can you see the spots on this baby puma?

Puma Dens

Mother pumas and their kittens live together in a den. When the kittens are about six months old, they leave the den to hunt with their mother. The kittens learn how to hunt by watching their mother.

Except for mothers with kittens, pumas live alone. Each puma travels across its own **home range** to look for food. **Solitary** pumas sometimes sleep in caves to escape bad weather, but they do not have fixed dens.

Pumas sometimes go into caves to get out of the rain or the sun.

Pumas and People

Pumas most often stay away from people. It is **rare** to see a puma in the wild. If you do see a puma, you should be careful. They are strong animals that can hurt or kill a person.

Do not go up to a puma. Stand back and leave room for the puma to move away from you. Keep facing the puma. Raise your arms so that you look bigger.

Pumas have strong, sharp teeth. This is one reason you should never fight with a puma.

Endangered Pumas

   People sometimes build houses and businesses on land where pumas live. When this happens the pumas and the people who live near them can cause problems for each other. Though pumas hardly ever **attack** people, they sometimes catch and eat people's pets or farm animals.

   When people have taken over most of the land, the pumas have no place to live and hunt. Pumas that live in places where there are many people may become **endangered**.

Glossary

attack (uh-TAK) To start a fight with.

endangered (in-DAYN-jerd) Describing a kind of animal that has almost died out.

habitats (HA-beh-tats) The kinds of land where an animal or a plant naturally lives.

hiss (HIS) To make a sound like when you say the letter "s."

home range (HOHM RAYNJ) The land on which an animal regularly stays.

leap (LEEP) A jump.

predators (PREH-duh-terz) Animals that kill other animals for food.

prey (PRAY) An animal that is hunted by another animal for food.

rare (RER) Not common.

scientists (SY-un-tists) People who study the world.

solitary (SAH-leh-ter-ee) Spending most time alone.

subspecies (SUB-spee-sheez) Different kinds of the same animal.

whiskers (HWIS-kerz) Hard hairs that grow on a face.

yowl (YOW-ul) To make a long, sad cry.

Index

Web Sites

Due to the changing nature of Internet links, PowerKids Press has developed an online list of Web sites related to this book. This site is updated regularly. Please use this link to access the list:
www.powerkidslinks.com/dcats/pumas/